The Execution

The Execution
Marie~Claire Blais
Translated by David Lobdell

Vancouver, Talonbooks, 1976

Published with assistance from the Canada Council.

Talonbooks
P.O. Box 2076, Vancouver, British Columbia, Canada V6B 3S3
www.talonbooks.com

Printed and bound in Canada by Hignell Book Printing.

Third Printing: August 2002

First published by Les Éditions du jour Inc., Montréal, Québec.

Canadian Cataloguing in Publication Data

Blais, Marie-Claire, 1939–
   [l'exécution. English]
   The Execution

   Translation of L'exécution.
   ISBN 0-88922-103-0

   I. Title.
PS8503   C842'.5'4   C77-002019-4
PR3919.B6E913

L'Exécution was first performed at Théâtre du Rideau Vert in Montréal, Québec, on March 15, 1968, with the following cast:

Louis Kent	Daniel Gadouas
Stéphane Martin	André Bernier
Christian Ambre	Hubert Gagnon
Eric	Sylvain Tellier
D'Argenteuil	Marc Bellier
Lancelot	Hubert Piuze
Le Supérieur	Loic Le Gouriadec
La mère de Kent	Andrée Saint-Laurent
Hélène, soeur de Stéphane	Josée Beauregard
La mère d'Eric	Marcelle Pallascio
Choeur des Elèves	Denis Valois, Jean Archambault, Gaëtan Gladu, Jean-Guy D'Amour, Jean-François Bélanger, Rémi Déry, Dominique Boisvert, François Perro, André Gariépy
Le Batteur	Claude Dion

Directed by Yvette Brind'Amour
Designed by Hugo Wuetrich
Costumes by François Barbeau

Act One
Scene One

The room of LOUIS KENT and STEPHANE MARTIN in a private school for boys.

LOUIS KENT, STEPHANE MARTIN and CHRISTIAN AMBRE are seated about a table. The room is dimly lit.

KENT: *opening his dictionary at the table*
"LOT! An object used in deciding something by chance, FORTUNE, STAKE!" It says here: "Many Athenian magistrates were chosen by lot." The dye is cast, my friends, we shall choose our victim by lot!

CHRISTIAN: *irritated*
It's too easy.

KENT:
You keep quiet. You're not even awake yet. Your job is to write. I want the name of each student on a slip of paper.

He brusquely removes CHRISTIAN's hat and sets it on the table.

KENT:
> There, put the names in the hat. . . Your name and mine too, Ambre!

STEPHANE: *rising*
> Kent, you know I don't like this idea of yours. If I agreed to go along with you in this crazy scheme it was only to amuse myself a little in this prison, to exercise my imagination in some wild and romantic adventure. But your idea is too trivial, I don't like it.

KENT:
> Make sure you also include the name of our friend, Luther. Do as I say, Ambre. And hurry up, the bell is going to ring any minute.

> *Turning to STEPHANE.*

> Excuse me, I wasn't listening. What did you say?

STEPHANE:
> You know very well what I said.

KENT:
> Yes, but why should I listen to you when you bore me? Life is short, I can't give my attention to everything, you know. So what bit of interesting information did you have to impart to me this time?

STEPHANE:
> I'm willing to be your accomplice in a murder if the murder is an intelligent one, if our act has a certain grandeur and significance to it. But I'm not interested in defiling myself in some trivial prank. We can't choose someone by lot. We must be conscious of our acts. You're forgetting the rules, Kent.

KENT:

Is that right? Well, as you know, I'm not very good at following rules. And besides, it seems to me that we have no time now for dreaming.

To CHRISTIAN.

Mix the names well. In a matter of minutes, my friends, we shall gaze upon the smiling face of our victim.

STEPHANE:

You disgust me, both of you!

KENT:

Is it possible that you're afraid of death?

STEPHANE:

It's not right. We should kill someone who is guilty, a priest for his scandalous behavior, a student who is consumed with vice, someone like that. Once again, you're breaking the rules.

KENT:

We are all consumed with vice. That's how it is.

To AMBRE.

What time is it?

CHRISTIAN:

Ten past six.

STEPHANE:

You too would be afraid to die at the hand of your best friend.

KENT:

Not at all.

Pause.

KENT:

And besides, you're not my best friend... My best friend is this fat little fellow here, Christian Ambre. Isn't that right, Ambre?

CHRISTIAN:
You're making fun of me. You're being mean.

KENT:

Oh yes, very mean. But listen, Ambre, life is going to be very good to us, you'll see. A comfortable little crime. You'll go on eating three times a day, and I'll go on preparing for my exams. A little shudder of horror from time to time perhaps... but you'll pay no attention to that...

STEPHANE:
You too would be frightened if you suddenly felt yourself being betrayed by the monster that lurks within you.

KENT:

What monster are you talking about? I'm afraid I'm not familiar with it. I'm lucky, you see. I'm light. As light as a bird. I've never felt so good.

CHRISTIAN:
The bell is going to ring any minute.

KENT:

Alright then, we must hurry. Who knows, perhaps Luther wants to go to mass this morning?

To STEPHANE.

What a fine hypocrite you are with all your pious poses! You know what your problem is? You're sentimental. It makes no difference that you might agree

10

to commit a murder. . . Inside, you never change. You nurse your guilt, you suppress your anger by appealing to the mercy of God. What a disgrace!

CHRISTIAN:

The names are all in the hat.

KENT:

Alright, Luther, the choice is yours. You have only to close your eyes and to select one of the slips. It's not difficult, disappointingly simple even for a dreamer like you, pining for the opportunity to kill a great man, a prince, some such remarkable creature. I always told you: murder too has its limitations. You have to accept that. Well, did you hear me? What are you waiting for?

STEPHANE:

I don't want to do it.

KENT:

I can do it myself, if you like. I can choose your name.

STEPHANE:

Our friendship means nothing to you then?

KENT:

We'll talk of that later. This is a moment for action.

STEPHANE:

None of this makes any sense. You want to destroy everything, don't you, even that private dream we had?

KENT:

My memory is not so good. What dream are you talking about?

STEPHANE:
The dream we talked about the night we were reading Goethe. . .

KENT: *interrupting him*
Oh, please don't bore me with your memories.

The bell rings. There is a moment of silence.

We have no time to waste, my friends. Everything must be completed before breakfast. You'll bring the victim to us, Ambre. We'll wait for you here, fortifying ourselves on sour milk. I don't want to leave Luther alone for a single moment. He's apt to report us to the Superior. Or to get himself secretly drunk. Isn't that right, Stéphane?

STEPHANE:
Listen, Louis. . .

Pause.

Oh, what's the use? You refuse to understand.

KENT:
Now you're talking sense. Bring the hat, Christian.

STEPHANE hesitates for a moment before drawing a slip from the hat. Standing behind him, KENT watches him impatiently.

Well, is it so difficult?

STEPHANE: *closing his eyes*
There, it's done.

Pause.

I won't read it.

KENT:
>Read it, Christian Ambre.

STEPHANE:
>Wait. I think I heard a noise. . .

KENT:
>Hurry up, Christian Ambre.

CHRISTIAN: *surprised*
>Eric!

STEPHANE:
>Eric Geoffroy?

KENT: *pleased*
>Eric? "Prince Eric?"

>*Pause.*

>Well, what are you waiting for, Ambre? Go and get him.

STEPHANE:
>No, wait. Let me choose another name. Eric has just arrived in our school. He's only a child. We can't kill a child.

KENT:
>A prince just for you, Luther! Prince Eric, straight out of our adventure stories. Ah! adolescence, how pure! How romantic! "The Death of Prince Eric". . . That's it!

STEPHANE:
>He's only fourteen. We can't do that.

KENT:
>Innocent too. . . An innocent little boy!

Pause.

KENT:

Bring him quickly, Ambre. I'm anxious to see this child.

STEPHANE: *trying to prevent AMBRE from leaving the room* Kent, I'll do anything for you, you know that, but don't ask me to kill Eric. Let it be someone else, you or me or one of these mediocre creatures we live amongst, but don't ask me to kill an innocent child, I can't do it. If you have any respect at all for yourself or for me. . .

KENT:

I have no respect for myself or for you. God, how you bore me! All this for some insignificant little student!

STEPHANE:

Can't you wait. . . until tomorrow?

KENT:

No.

STEPHANE:

Until tonight then?

KENT:

No. But I tell you what I will do. . . Just for you, I'll wait until mass is over. Does that make you feel any better?

> *STEPHANE steps sadly aside. AMBRE leaves. KENT stops him in the doorway and whispers something in his ear, then returns to the room.*

I do everything to accommodate you. I told him to wait until after communion.

STEPHANE:
I'm afraid for you, Kent.

The student choir can be heard singing mass in the chapel. STEPHANE stands near the door, an anxious look on his face.

Speak to me. I can't stand your silence. What are you writing in that book?

KENT:
Notes. I'm making plans. I'm trying to think.

STEPHANE:
We must decide what we are going to do with. . .

KENT:
With our victim?

STEPHANE: *ashamed*
Yes.

KENT:
I've worked that all out. I give the orders, you follow them.

STEPHANE:
What do I gain from being your accomplice? You hide everything from me; your plans, your intentions, everything. That doesn't bring us any closer, you know. You can't imagine how much importance I attached to this act which we were to perform together. . . I. . .

KENT:
Romantic!

STEPHANE:
Listen. . . They're singing the Kyrie. There's still time to change our plans, Kent. It was a crazy idea anyway, it was a nightmare, there's still time to put

a stop to it. We can think of some other fate for
Eric. . . Yes, we can take him to the theatre on
Thursday, I have an extra ticket. . .

KENT:
Offer him your ticket then. I'm sure he'll be touched.

Pause.

In fact, that might not be such a bad idea. We should
always be kind to those who are about to die.

STEPHANE:
I don't want to have anything to do with this
disgusting act.

KENT:
There's nothing disgusting about it, Luther. Nothing
at all. No blood to clean up. No weapon to conceal.
A sharp blow of the hand to the back of the neck.
Like this!

*He raises his hand in the air and feigns a blow to
someone's neck.*

Eric collapses quietly on the table. It's over. Do you
still call that a disgusting act? A little adventure of
the utmost simplicity!

STEPHANE:
I thought you were capable of something more noble
than this, Louis.

KENT: *mocking STEPHANE*
What language! "Oh, Louis, I thought you were
capable of something more noble than this,
something more courageous, something a little less
stingy!" Well, I am stingy, I tell you. You're certainly
the more generous of us, I grant you that. And then,
of course, you love the luxury of weapons, blood,
the gory print of a knife on human flesh. You are in

16

love with the glory of killing, my friend, but you are no true killer.

STEPHANE:

What am I then to have followed you so far?

KENT:

A faithful friend, I admit it. You are remarkably loyal.

STEPHANE:

At such a serious moment, you joke, you make fun of me. You're so arrogant you even find pleasure in someone else's death.

KENT:

What a preacher you are, Luther! Yes, I'm enjoying myself. But I take my pleasures coolly, I savour them, while you stand there trembling with fear. Oh, all those fine words of yours, all those fine promises to follow me right to the end, to be my devoted disciple, the humble servant of all my smallest desires! And now look at you! It's disgusting! Before I know it, you'll be as weak as Christian Ambre, nothing but a pathetic little accomplice. . .

STEPHANE:

What proof do you need then of my friendship?

KENT:

The ultimate proof, you know that.

STEPHANE:

You're asking too much of me. I can't go through with this, not without the help of. . . the protection of. . . a weapon, not without. . .

KENT:

That is precisely how mediocre people kill! With a taste for blood on their lips! With a feverish frenzy inflating their hearts!

He laughs.

KENT:

Well, I won't allow it. Everything must happen as normally as possible. Christian Ambre will bring Eric to us. We'll invite him to join us for coffee. In that way, we'll put him at his ease. We'll talk about the exams, the teachers, our Greek translations, things like that. We won't make our move until mass is over. When you hear the Amen, that will be the signal. You'll be standing behind this chair.

He shows STEPHANE the spot.

I'll say, "A ticket for Phaedre, Eric?"... I'll repeat the question... That will be your cue. Your prince will lean forward, his pale neck will be exposed... *You'll strike... a single blow... like that!*

Pause.

Remember, your hand is a knife, an axe, some object that takes its strength from you. But I've taught you all that, you can't have forgotten it already... Do you understand? When you hear the question, "A ticket for Phaedre, Eric?" you make your move. Eric collapses without a sound on the table. It's over.

Long pause.

And what will we do with the body? I've thought of that too. You can't imagine how well I've planned this whole thing. All my reading has not been in vain, you know...

STEPHANE:

Please, don't tell me any more. I don't want to hear it. We'll talk of that later.

KENT:

Later? But you must be mad! Everything must be planned in advance! This is the part which excites me the most. A true mathematical problem, a game of the utmost simplicity and skill, you can't imagine!

STEPHANE:

I'll look after the body myself. And I'll do it in a more humane way than you ever would. After all, Eric will be my victim, not yours.

KENT:

I believe you're suffering from illusions, my little preacher-friend. The entire production will be mine. From beginning to end. It is already mine. It is my strength which crushes Eric like an insect. And I don't even have to raise a hand. . .

STEPHANE:

Eric will be my victim because it is I who will be responsible for his death. Because it is I who will kill him.

KENT:

No! That's your self-indulgent way of looking at things, but you don't understand. I always did say you were inferior to me. What an idiotic inclination it was on my part to ally myself with a nonentity like you! In the end, you're worth no more than the rest of them. I judged you on the brilliance of your note taking, on the striking quality of your appearance. I must have been mad. I shall always be my own master, my disciples have nothing to teach me, I have no interest in them whatever. I am the only one of you who is capable of taking a life, of imposing his will upon others. All you will ever be good for is writing poems, I'm afraid.
And I told you that you would have to renounce everything for me. I had only one dream for you, Stéphane, to elevate you, to raise you to some great spiritual height. . . Yes, a great Nietzschean

dream. . . The anguish of life and death at their
summit. . .

STEPHANE: *upset*
> I renounced a great deal for you. I'll never write
> another poem. I'll never read another book. Didn't
> I renounce my entire life to follow you? What more
> do you want?

KENT:
> Take it easy. Let me explain. . . At seven-fifteen,
> I'll take up the watch in the corridor, I'll see to it
> that no one observes the three of you as you leave
> for your morning walk, you and Christian Ambre
> holding Eric by the arms and dragging him toward
> the stairway, as if he were drunk or slightly ill.
> You'll go down to the yard, I'll be waiting for you
> there. Then you'll walk towards the woods, with Eric
> between you. He won't be heavy, he's only a child.
> You'll wait for me under the tree where we usually
> meet. I'll join you there. Then, we'll walk to the
> centre of the woods and bury Eric beneath the trees.
> We must be back here before noon, in time for the
> midday meal. We'll come in at the sound of the bell,
> as usual. We must think of everything. We may
> be questioned about our absence from chapel.
> We'll say that we were here in my room, studying
> for the exams. Tomorrow morning, Christian Ambre
> will be the first to speak to the Superior about Eric's
> disappearance. That will establish our innocence. . .

STEPHANE:
> They'll see our tracks in the snow. They'll find out. . .
> Yes, someday, they'll find out everything. . .

KENT:
> No, it's snowing. It's going to snow all day.

STEPHANE:
> We can't bury Eric beneath the trees.

KENT:

What do you suggest then? Do you have a better solution?

STEPHANE:

We'll leave Eric in the bushes. And then tonight, we'll take him to the cemetery and give him a decent burial.

KENT:

You're a character straight out of a tragedy, aren't you? You want Eric to rest peacefully amongst the dead. How pure you are!

STEPHANE:

That's all I ask. If you won't come with me, then I'll do it myself.

KENT:

I'm afraid you'll have to. I don't like cemeteries. And besides, as you said, Eric will be your responsibility, not mine...

STEPHANE:

And if the truth comes out?

KENT:

The truth rarely comes out, alas. Don't worry about it.

STEPHANE:

We'll be caught... Yes, perhaps not today or tomorrow, but one day, you'll see, I'll be caught, I'll be charged.

KENT:

I've thought of that too. In fact the idea doesn't exactly displease me. You would become the centre of attention for a change. A little glory might do you good, you seem to be rather in the shade these days.

STEPHANE:
Our classmates may be vile and contemptible in your
eyes, but not one of them would agree to kill
someone as I have done today.

KENT:
That remains to be seen. They need only be given
the idea.

STEPHANE:
What do you mean?

KENT:
We could bewitch them, let them in on the secret.
Oh, I can see them now, all of them, coming to laugh
and joke with me about this murder. . .

STEPHANE:
Isn't it bad enough that we've involved ourselves
in such an ugly business without contaminating the
entire class? I don't understand your attitude, Kent.
We spoke of a gratuitous murder, a private murder,
not some perverse atrocity that would be broadcast
all over the school.

KENT:
You speak of *my* attitude. Well, it seems to me, my
friend, that *your* attitude is becoming more and more
hypocritical. You try to qualify things, to make
distinctions, but that doesn't change a thing, you
know. The act remains precisely the same.

STEPHANE:
If you only knew how frightened I am. . .

KENT:
Things will go better the second time.

STEPHANE:
What? You mean to do it again?

KENT:
Why not?

STEPHANE:
You already feel compelled to... the need to...
to...?

KENT:
A first crime is a rather humiliating experience, don't
you agree? One must proceed quickly to the second.

STEPHANE:
Just like that, in cold blood, you could...?

KENT:
I'm eighteen years old. Life is just opening itself
up to me, my adventures are only beginning. Why
shouldn't I enjoy myself a little?

Mocking STEPHANE.

Let us drink from the cup of cold dark pleasures,
my friend! From the cup of danger and gloom!

STEPHANE: *a little captivated*
I remember last year you were onstage, playing the
roles of Oedipus and Creon. You thought you were
alone. You cried in a triumphant voice: "O, woe is
me, may I die damned if I have done this thing of
which you accuse me!" Your eyes glowed savagely.
I was watching you from the wings. Even then
you were playing at being someone else. You were
acting, yes, just as today you act at murder. You
frightened me. I thought "Is this really Louis Kent,
is this really the one I have chosen to follow?" For
I sensed already that you were going to lead me into
a dark, dangerous universe, and you were the only

one who was capable of exciting me like that, of captivating me with your dreams:

"Do not denounce and disgrace without proof
The one who has pledged his allegiance by oath. . ."

The words you spoke touched my heart.

KENT:

Because *you* had a heart.

STEPHANE:

I was proud then, and strong. And now look at me, cringing like an animal. Oh, what a friend! What an oath! This is what comes of having listened to you so eagerly on that day on the verge of some terrible folly! For is there any difference between the one who takes a single life and the one who takes ten? Between the one who kills a child and the one who kills an old man? You're right, Kent, no difference at all, not a shade of difference! Do you know what we're becoming? The enemies of life! Joyful assasins! If I'm capable of killing Eric this morning, I'll be capable of killing you tonight. It no longer makes any difference, you see. You might actually die at my hand, have you thought of that?

KENT:

Anything is possible, my friend. I might also betray you in front of the entire class, yes, I might deliver you up to their loud approval, to their rude laughter, to that vulgar complicity which lies dormant within each one of us and which is so easily awakened. . . I might do that, you know. You are entirely in my hands.

STEPHANE:

Yes, Kent, anything is possible now. . . Nothing is certain anymore. . .

CHRISTIAN AMBRE enters, holding ERIC by the arm. The boy is smiling. STEPHANE and KENT shake him by the hand and invite him to sit.

KENT:

So, Prince Eric, will you join us for coffee? It's cold in here, isn't it? Close the door, Christian. Well, how are you, Eric? Working hard? I had you brought here so I could make a few inquiries about your studies. . .

ERIC: *simply*
I'm fine, thank you.

KENT:

You're shy, eh? Why's that? Because you're new here? Well, you'll get over it, I was the same in the beginning, I blushed the moment anyone spoke to me. This is the first time you've been in here, isn't it? This is our Saturday meeting place. Don't tell the Superior about it though, he might cut short our holidays. You're pale, you look tired, have you been working too hard?

ERIC:

No, I'm fine, thank you.

KENT:

You don't know me, I'm the president of the class, yes, I am personally responsible for our large family. Stéphane is my vice-president, and Ambre, my secretary.

Pause.

We need some information from you.

Pause.

Is it alright if I take notes while we talk?

25

ERIC:
> Yes, of course.

KENT:
> You arrived on the twelfth of November, I believe.
> Is that right?

ERIC:
> Yes.

KENT:
> Do you like our school?

ERIC:
> Yes. But I don't like all the bars on the windows.

KENT:
> You mustn't complain. A rigourous education makes
> for a rigourous spirit.

> *Turning to STEPHANE.*

> Isn't that right, Luther?

CHRISTIAN: *curtly*
> And discipline is good for the soul.

KENT:
> So, you're studying the piano, is that right?

ERIC:
> Yes.

KENT:
> I see, I see.

STEPHANE:
> But what do you see?

KENT:
> That everything is going just as I planned.

To ERIC.

You sing in the choir?

ERIC:

Yes.

KENT:

We're going to have a beautiful midnight mass this year. Will you go home after the mass?

STEPHANE:

This is all so pointless. We're supposed to be questioning Eric about his studies.

KENT:

My friend wants me to ask you what you plan to do when you grow up. As if you were still a little boy. But I see a book in your pocket, what is it?

ERIC:

"Prince Eric."

KENT:

Oh, so you're reading "The Adventures of Prince Eric?"

ERIC:

No, it's the final volume, "The Death of Prince Eric." I read "The Death of Prince Eric" every winter.

KENT:

Very interesting.

Pause.

Tell me, did you take communion this morning?

STEPHANE:

That's a personal question, Kent.

KENT:
Do you often take communion?

ERIC:
Everyday.

KENT:
Indeed? Because your spiritual director advised it?

ERIC:
No, because I want to. But I don't like going to confession.

KENT:
Shocking! We are all in need of divine purification. You as well as the rest of us.

Throwing his head in the air.

"Lead him not into temptation, Father, deliver him from evil."

STEPHANE:
Eric, we brought you here to. . .

KENT: *interrupting*
To cheer you up a little. Yes, I've seen you in chapel and in study hall. You looked rather sad. Aren't you happy here?

ERIC:
I'm fine, thank you.

STEPHANE:
Eric, we thought that. . .

KENT:
That you might like to go out next Thursday evening. Yes, a little diversion might be good for you.

ERIC:

Thank you, but I can't go out next Thursday evening.

KENT:

Because of your studies?

ERIC:

Yes.

STEPHANE: *awkwardly*

I thought you might like to go to the show with me. There's a good film playing at. . .

KENT:

Oh, Luther, stop babbling! Let's get down to business!

STEPHANE:

I don't feel well. I'm going outside for a few minutes.

KENT:

It can wait. Sit down please.

STEPHANE:

Mass will soon be over. Let me go, Kent.

KENT:

Impossible. Now we must speak of more serious matters. Eric, what were you doing in the yard yesterday morning at seven o'clock with Pierre d'Argenteuil?

ERIC:

At seven o'clock? But I was still in bed, I think.

KENT:

Come now, think carefully.

ERIC:

I wasn't up yet. You can ask the brother who was on supervision. I had a sore throat. I was in bed.

KENT:
I wonder if the brother who was on supervision might be a liar. I wonder if you might be.

ERIC: *calmly*
I was in bed.

STEPHANE:
Wake up, Eric. Open your eyes. Can't you see what...

CHRISTIAN:
I saw you in the yard yesterday morning at seven o'clock. With Pierre d'Argenteuil. You're aware of the reputation of Pierre d'Argenteuil, aren't you?

ERIC:
No. Why?

CHRISTIAN:
You haven't heard the things that are said about him?

ERIC:
People say wicked things, it's true. But I don't listen to them...

Pause.

Ask the Superior. He'll tell you I was in bed.

CHRISTIAN:
We don't tolerate things like that here, Eric Geoffroy. Your conduct has been found questionable by the president and his secretary. That is why we have brought you here.

STEPHANE:
No, Eric, no...

KENT:
Tell the truth. I won't scold you.

ERIC:

I don't know what you're talking about. I was sleeping, I was in bed.

KENT:

Perhaps you're a sleepwalker.

ERIC:

If I'm a sleepwalker, I don't know about it. It's possible though.

CHRISTIAN:

So it's possible that you got up in your sleep?

ERIC:

But I was asleep. A person can't do anything wrong in his sleep.

KENT:

Oh, I'm not so sure about that!

Pause.

You're blushing, why?

ERIC:

I'm tired.

CHRISTIAN:

He's blushing with shame, that's what!

ERIC:

I want to go to my room now.

KENT: *preventing him from rising*
No, no. You can't leave just like that. That would be too easy. You don't walk away from a trial so easily, you know. So, it's true, Pierre d'Argenteuil is your friend?

ERIC:

We do our algebra together. He's very kind to me.

KENT:

What an angel you are! You call that kind. . .

ERIC:

Pierre d'Argenteuil helps me with my Latin.

KENT:

How shocking! What is happening in this school?
No moral integrity, everyone giving in to his instincts!
Here I was under the impression that I was living
in a clean, wholesome place. . . And what do I find
all about me? Evil! Vice!

STEPHANE:

Stop it, I don't want to hear any more of this!

KENT:

A little respect, Luther, if you please. I'm speaking.

Scornfully.

You are aware of my devotion to good causes, you
should be a little more respectful. I am only thinking
of the good reputation of our school, of its public
image. I don't have to tell you that morality is a
solid terrain upon which one can walk without mis-
giving or fear!

ERIC:

You can ask the Superior if you want. I was sleeping.
But a person can be a sleepwalker without knowing
it. If you saw me in the yard, it must have been because I was sleepwalking.

KENT:

You were walking. . . alone?

ERIC:

With Pierre d'Argenteuil perhaps, since I was asleep!

KENT:

And you admit that you have done this thing for which we hold you responsible?

ERIC:

What thing?

CHRISTIAN:

I saw you, don't try to trick us. I wrote it all down in my book. Nothing is missing. The president of the class was not familiar with your story. The report which I gave him of your conduct has deeply disturbed him. There is only one solution, to remove you from the list. To remove your name.

ERIC:

What list are you talking about?

CHRISTIAN:

The list of students, what else? You might contaminate the others with your vice. The list of the living, it's simple. As secretary of the class, I must also look after the moral integrity of the students.

STEPHANE:

We live in a den of iniquity and you speak of moral integrity! You make me laugh. . .

KENT:

Be quiet, Stéphane.

STEPHANE:

I'll tell the truth! I'm the one who deserves to be accused, not Eric. . . I'm a hypocrite, I take advantage of those who are weaker than I. I'm a liar, I'm a cheat. . .

KENT:
Be quiet, I said. Your confession doesn't interest us.

ERIC: *suddenly upset*
I want to leave.

CHRISTIAN:
Just one moment. It won't be long now. The mass is almost over.

ERIC:
Why did you bring me here?

KENT: *scornfully*
To rape you, my child.

Pause.

Let's be serious now. What time is it, Ambre?

CHRISTIAN:
Five past seven.

KENT:
Don't be frightened, Prince Eric, we aren't dangerous, we aren't going to hurt you. Smile, come on, that's it, what a nice little boy you are! I like you very much, you know. I'm going to forgive you this time. But Pierre d'Argenteuil will be punished.

ERIC:
I want to go.

KENT:
Promise me that you'll stay away from him in the future.

ERIC:
Let me go.

KENT:

In a few moments, we shall take a short walk together.

CHRISTIAN:

As far as the cemetery, if you like.

KENT:

Do you have a message to send to your family before we go, or a letter to write?

ERIC: *gazing fearfully about him, as if he suddenly understood everything* Let me go! Let me go!

KENT:

You don't have a dear little sister you'd like to write to before we leave? You never know, you might get lost during your walk. . .

ERIC: *in a small, pleading voice*
Mother!

KENT:

Oh, what a dear little boy! He thinks of his mother. I always forget mine. What an angel you are! You're not the only one who loves his mother, you know.

STEPHANE: *upset*
Hélène!

KENT:

Stéphane! How strange! What's come over you, calling your sister like that? You're forgetting yourself, you're switching roles. It's just as I thought, you want the sort of attention that is reserved for victims. . .

ERIC:

Let me go! Let me go!

KENT:

Calm down, child. Come now, don't look at me like that. Do you see what I have for you? A ticket for Thursday night. We were just joking. You didn't understand?

Long pause.

Yes, it was just a game. It's what we call initiation. So now, you're really one of us. You have been initiated into fear.

ERIC:

A game. . . It's true?

KENT:

Yes, a game. Prince Eric. It's done in all the schools.

ERIC:

I thought you wanted to kill me.

KENT:

Silly boy!

CHRISTIAN:

Do you feel better now?

ERIC:

Yes, a little. I was scared. It seemed so real.

CHRISTIAN:

How could we kill you? We have no weapons here.

ERIC:

Yes, how could you?

KENT:

We're not savages, you know.

CHRISTIAN:
> You should be ashamed of yourself for thinking such things about your seniors.

KENT:
> And here's your reward. A ticket for Phaedre. . . Would you like a ticket for Phaedre, Eric?

> *Very quickly and somewhat to his own surprise, STEPHANE strikes ERIC on the neck. The child collapses.*

Scene Two

Several hours later, following the evening meal. The room is in a state of disorder. A lighted lamp sits on a pile of books. STEPHANE is asleep on KENT's bed; he is fully dressed. Near the bed, CHRISTIAN AMBRE is huddled on the floor, also asleep, his face hidden in the collar of his coat, his hat still on his head. KENT walks to and fro in the room, talking at times to himself, at times to his sleeping comrades. He moves from a state of violent passion to one of cold indifference, without once losing that strange quality of strength and dignity which CHRISTIAN and STEPHANE so admire in him. He is at once innocent, enigmatic and evil, as capable of feigning anger as gentleness. His roles varies constantly. . .

KENT: *reading from his notebook*
> "Here it is, recreation hour, and you sleep! But I rejoice, for I am about to organize a little celebration in honour of my great victory! This is a moment for rejoicing, and there you lie, Stéphane, sobbing in

37

your dreams. Oh what a pity, my friend! Amen. . .
Amen. . ."

In an ironic tone.

"I too offered a sacrifice on the altar this morning,
I discovered the great secret of blood without even
spilling it, and here I am, pure and innocent, like
the sacriligious priest who hides from the world the
dark prayer of his heart as he raises in his immaculate
hands the sacred host which he pretends to adore
but which his heart silently abjures. . ."

CHRISTIAN: *as if calling from afar in his sleep*
Kent. . . Oh Kent. . .

KENT:
You ate tonight without remorse, Christian Ambre.
You glutted yourself at the feast. But my appetite
is not yet appeased. Someone is waiting for me
somewhere. Someone is dreaming of submitting
himself to me. Of obeying me. The submission of
others shall be my daily bread, their sufferings,
their humiliations, the rich wine with which I am
already steeped. . . You are nothing but a vulgar
glutton, a sleepy little scavenger, you have the quick
hunger of a wolf; but I am like the eagle that sits
on a lonely peak, patiently awaiting its prey, constantly postponing the attack in order better to
revel in its lordly pride.

Pause.

Wake up, Christian Ambre, tell me what happened,
I see bloodstains on your coat. . .

He shakes Christian but cannot arouse him.

I can imagine what you did. It's cowards like you
who seek the shadows of night in order to give
themselves up to carnage. When I left you beneath

the trees, you defiled the purity of our act by smashing Eric's skull with the shovel you carried in your hand. . . Wake up, I know you can hear me, isn't that what you did?

STEPHANE: *awakening with a start and rising*
Yes, Kent, that's what I did.

KENT: *calmly*
Stéphane, you're tired. It's been a long day for you. You must try to get a little more sleep, there's still an hour before study hall.

STEPHANE:
Listen to me, Kent. I must tell you the truth. I didn't have the courage to bury him. He's still there, in the bushes. There is blood on the snow.

KENT:
Take it easy.

STEPHANE:
I thought he was dead. But he was only stunned. We carried him between us, he was very light, his feet barely touched the snow. . . Suddenly, I felt his breath on my cheek. He spoke to me, he said, "Thank you, I'm fine, thank you." I think that's what he said to me. . .

KENT:
You're delirious. Eric was dead.

STEPHANE:
No, he was still alive. I felt his breath on my hand again when Christian and I laid him beneath the trees. He spoke to me. I heard him.

KENT:
You should know that things like this often happen at such moments. You have visions, you hear voices, it's normal. It's as if you were under the influence

of a strong drug. I warned you that something like this might happen, didn't I? Calm down now. Go back to sleep. There's nothing to fear. We won't be bothered for a few hours yet.

STEPHANE:
He's out there, I can't leave him out there like that.

KENT:
It's your remorse that you can't leave.

STEPHANE:
I lost a friend before I had a chance to know him. I can hear him calling me from the woods. . .

KENT:
Oh, you'll never be anything but a poet! Your weakness disgusts me!

STEPHANE:
Christian Ambre, wake up! You're a monster! I was standing beside you, I couldn't move, I was terrified, I was paralyzed with shame. You said, "He's not dead, let's kill him." And you struck him. . . again. . . and again. . . You lost control of yourself and you struck him on the head and his blood ran out on the snow, I was there and I didn't say a word. I watched you. Once again, I just stood there and watched.

KENT: *touching STEPHANE's shoulder*
Listen my friend, you must gain control of yourself. Come, sit down. I am innocent. You two are the guilty ones. Only my innocence can protect you now. I am going to take you under my protection. Trust me, I'll look after you. I know what is best.

STEPHANE:
But how. . . How can speak of your innocence after all that? You're the one who did it all.

KENT:
Me, really?

STEPHANE:
Yes, you, Louis Kent. The real murderer is you. You are responsible for everything.

KENT:
Did I make a single move?

STEPHANE:
No. I guess, in a certain sense, you don't have the courage to be guilty. You leave the guilt and the fear to us. You don't even have the courage to act. All you can do is to incite others to perform the horrible deeds which you can't bring yourself to perform.

KENT:
You're very wise, Luther, you understand how it is. You still preach a little too much for my taste, but I forgive you for that. . . It's true that your guilt fortifies my innocence, and your shame, my pride. That is the mechanism of horror. I direct that mechanism from afar. I do the thinking, I make the decisions. And you are nothing but one of those common little wheels that is used for awhile and then rejected.

Pause.

But don't get upset over that. Look at this smart little fellow here. Christian Ambre. They should have called him Christian Ombre. You know what *ombre* means, don't you?. . . *Shadow.* Your shadow and mine, Stéphane. And look, he sleeps. I doubt that he even remembers. . . It is people like him I dream of wiping from the face of the earth, those who sleep!

STEPHANE:

How can you speak of those who sleep, you who
have no conscience, you who sleep a sleep far deeper
and more cruel than any human sleep... Because, as
I was closing Eric's eyes, it seemed to me that
you had stripped me of my soul, yes, I had the
distinct impression that my soul had suddenly
dropped away from me...

KENT:

Let's not concern ourselves with something that
doesn't exist. The soul! If anything makes me happy,
it is not to have one...

STEPHANE:

Your crime is a lack of conscience. Simply that.
There is no greater crime.

KENT:

How I love you and your little sermons, your
accusations, your complaints! You're so irresistible.
Here, let me embrace you!

STEPHANE: *pushing him aside*
Keep away from me!

KENT:

But that's impossible, you know, we have never
been so close.

STEPHANE:

It's time to stop acting, Kent. There is only one way
for us to get ourselves out of this situation now
with any honour and dignity... Suicide.

KENT:

You've been reading too many books, my friend.
I can see that I haven't kept close enough watch
over you.

STEPHANE:

I don't feel any contempt for you, Kent, not anymore. Something tells me that you're blind and that one day you'll open your eyes to the full horror of this situation. Something tells me that when that happens, you will want to cry, like a child, but that it will be too late. . .

KENT:

To put it simply. . . You pity me?

STEPHANE:

Perhaps, yes, that's all that's left to me now, it's little enough. Please don't destroy this fragile bond. We must die together, Kent. It's the only way to atone for Eric's death. We must do this before they begin to make investigations, before they discover Eric's body and bring it back here, before you are forced to recognize in each of his wounds your responsibility for this terrible crime.

KENT:

How complicated you are, you exhaust me! But I have no desire whatever to extricate myself from this situation. On the contrary, I intend to savour it. You can't imagine how much I enjoy long, protracted pleasures, as well as the anticipation, the suspense, that precede them! If you think I'd sacrifice my life for what you call honour, or whatever. . . Well, you're mistaken. I value myself too highly. It is only for my own pleasure that I would ever consent to die.

STEPHANE:

Alright then, since you refuse. . .

KENT:

Can you imagine the scene of our death? Our redemptive death, as you call it? They would find our bodies here in the morning, entwined together, the Superior would cry scandal, the students would flock to witness the tragic spectacle: the disciples of honour lying together on the floor, my head resting on your shoulder. Mysterious suicide, questions would be asked, rumours would abound. For several weeks, they would talk of the two handsome young men who had everything, intelligence, talent, breeding, who lacked nothing, no, nothing. People would shake their heads in bewilderment. Why on earth would they kill themselves? Then the Superior would issue a statement to the effect that the wages of sin are death and that the suicide of Louis Kent and Stéphane Martin is the sure proof of that. We would serve as a lesson to the other students in the school. Masses would be said for the repose of our souls. . .

Pause.

Does the prospect of that little drama please you?

STEPHANE:
It's impossible for you to speak of a thing without corrupting it with the baseness of your words. That's exactly how you spoke to Eric this morning. But he didn't understand you. Your language is so impure that it takes a person at least as depraved as yourself to understand it.

KENT:
Let me add that you seem to understand it very well.

STEPHANE:
I must have been mad to suggest that we die together. You would have let me poison myself alone. Once again, you would have been deceitful enough to pretend to poison yourself and. . .

KENT:
You're learning, my friend. That's exactly what I would have done. I would have acted out the scene of my death and then watched you die alone.

Pause.

Oh Stéphane, that was just a bad joke, You know very well that I couldn't live without you. How could I survive without your will to guide me, your insight to enlighten me? I'm a passionless brute. I have no heart. I need your heart in my breast to keep me alive.

STEPHANE:

If I didn't think you were still acting, your words would move me very deeply.

KENT:

But I'm not acting, I'm quite sincere. That's rare, you know. You should appreciate it.

STEPHANE:

You're acting, I know it.

KENT:

Here, let me embrace you as a sign of our reconciliation. You too have become hard, you know, yes, as hard as a stone. You obeyed me this morning without enthusiasm. Before long, I'm afraid you're going to begin to despise me.

STEPHANE:

No, Kent, no more acting. I've had enough of your theatrical gestures. Keep away from me. From now on, I'm on my own.

KENT:

I'm going to show you how much I care for you. Yes, I'm going to enhance your reputation in the eyes of the class, I'm going to give you a name in this school. You will become our hero, our triumph, our glory!

STEPHANE:

Nothing can touch me now.

KENT:

I knew this would happen. But it will pass, Stéphane. You'll get used to it, you'll accustom yourself to living with the murderer that lies within you. Look, Christian Ambre has already accustomed himself to it. And he sleeps.

STEPHANE:

I'll never sleep again.

KENT:

That too will pass, you'll see. It's just like an illness. You always recuperate. You're not the only one to have known these anxious hours which follow a crime. We try to hide from ourselves, but we always end up by coming back to ourselves, we find ourselves again, and we discover that we're more at home with ourselves than we ever were. We discover new qualities in ourselves. Tomorrow morning, when you awaken, you will feel amazing strengths rising within you, you will feel noble, triumphant, as mighty as a king. . .

STEPHANE:

That death should strike me down, that I should vanish forever from the face of the earth. . . That's what I should wish for, Louis! Nothing else!

KENT:

You can't kill yourself, Luther. You can't vanish. You promised to stand by me, remember.

STEPHANE:

Those were the words of a person in distress. They can be revoked.

KENT:

And then. . . there's Hélène.

STEPHANE:

No!

KENT:

At the moment of the crime, you called out to her, you cried out to that little girl. She wasn't there, but you appealed to her all the same, you turned to her instead of me.

STEPHANE:

That didn't prevent me from killling Eric.

KENT:

What got into you?

STEPHANE:

I don't know. For a moment, it almost seemed that Hélène was the victim. I suddenly saw her in the place of Eric.

KENT:

You're still too complicated for me.

STEPHANE:

I understood suddenly all the pain I would be inflicting upon her. I appealed to Hélène to help me, to protect me from myself.

KENT:

And the proof that you have no soul is that Hélène did not help you, that you struck Eric. . . In a masterly fashion, I might add, he dropped like a stone. What skill! What strength! You even had me frightened for a moment.

STEPHANE:

Eric is dead. Hélène is alive. I shall be charged. And Hélène will have to bear my guilt for the rest of her life. She is my sister.

KENT:

You can always keep it from her.

STEPHANE:
No. In fact, I think she may already know it, I think she may have sensed it.

KENT:
It troubles me to see you so tormented. I never knew you cared so much for your sister. . .

STEPHANE:
I forbid you even to mention her name.

KENT:
I'm terribly jealous.

STEPHANE:
Enough! No more!

KENT:
But its time to speak of practical things.

STEPHANE:
You and your practical things! The earth is opening up and you speak of practical things!

KENT:
Exactly, the earth is opening up. And that is why I'm not as happy as you think.

STEPHANE:
Let's not lay the blame for our behaviour upon the depraved state of the world, that would be too in-decent. You had everything going for you, Kent, you admitted as much yourself, you lacked nothing. Nothing. The majority of our classmates have known poverty and misery, but you and I never had one moment's suffering until we began to decay with boredom in this school. . . We were always saved, protected by our common indifference to life, we were of a separate race, you said, we were incapable of suffering, we were superior, we were noble, in-sensitive, proud. . .

KENT: *sarcastically*
And I had everything I could ever ask for, the adoration of my mother, the glowing respect of my father, the blind and fatuous love of my brothers and sisters. What was I lacking, if not a heart?

STEPHANE:
You lacked nothing, you had everything.

KENT:
I lack a heart. . . Is it not essential?

STEPHANE:
You've always been filled with scorn for everything and everyone. I remember that you were like that even as a child, you were tyrannical and abusive, and you haven't changed. People are fascinated by you, they are dazzled by your presence, but no one ever seems to have seen you as you really are. . .

KENT:
Fortunately, you came along to open my eyes, and I was able to see myself for the terrible monster I am. What a disappointment! What a deception!. . . The young man has toppled from his pedestal. He is wallowing in the mud. But strangely, he enjoys the mud. What is he to do?

STEPHANE:
Listen to me, Louis. Time is passing and Eric is still lying in the bushes, right where Christian and I left him, afraid that we might see him return to life before our very eyes. If we have any trace of dignity and sanity left in us, we must go now and bury him.

KENT:
Too late. Relax, my friend, it's too late.

CHRISTIAN: *suddenly awakening*
Prison! Prison! They're coming to get me!

Scene Three

*The dining room, eight o'clock the following
morning. LOUIS KENT has brought his classmates together to speak to them of the murder
of ERIC GEOFFROY. CHRISTIAN and
STEPHANE are absent. The students are eating.
KENT stands at the end of a long table. At
times, he seems almost to be alone onstage.
The students are no more to him than
silhouettes or shadows. We hear their voices
without always seeing their faces.*

KENT:

My friends, the Superior informed us this morning of
the disappearance of Eric Geoffroy. As president of
the class, I have brought you together to speak of
this matter.

Pause.

Did anyone here see Eric leave the school grounds
during the night?

D'ARGENTEUIL: *quickly*
I haven't seen Eric Geoffroy for two days.

KENT:

You are very quick to defend yourself. Why?

D'ARGENTEUIL:

Whenever a student disappears, I'm always accused
of having hidden him somewhere. That's why I
defend myself.

KENT:

We'll have a private talk later, you and I.

The students laugh.

Don't worry, imbecile, I wouldn't even take the trouble to blame you. I despise you too much. It is irresponsible people like you who are damned by God himself...

D'ARGENTEUIL:
What do you mean? Explain yourself...

KENT:
We don't want you here.

STUDENTS:
We don't want you here!

D'ARGENTEUIL:
Well, I don't understand...

KENT:
On the contrary, you understand very well. Let's not go into details. Everyone knows of your scandalous behaviour in this school. This is not the first time that an attractive child has disappeared...

D'ARGENTEUIL:
I'm not responsible for Eric's disappearance.

KENT:
Did I say that?

D'ARGENTEUIL:
You implied it.

KENT:
I just wanted to frighten you a little.

Pause.

Tell me, d'Argenteuil, did you see Eric Geoffroy Friday morning before mass?

51

D'ARGENTEUIL:
    Friday morning? Yes, I saw him in the dormitory.
    He had a sore throat. The Superior gave him
    permission to stay in bed.

KENT:
    Did you see him again during the day?

D'ARGENTEUIL:
    Yes, at ten o'clock. I gave him a lesson in Latin. He
    was late for the exam. I haven't seen him since.

KENT:
    That child confided in me. He thought very highly of
    you.

D'ARGENTEUIL:
    Why do you speak of him in the past tense?

KENT:
    Because he is no more.

D'ARGENTEUIL:
    Don't frighten us, Kent. Tell us where he's been
    hiding since yesterday. Was he beaten up by some
    of the older boys?

KENT:
    See how worried he is. . .

STUDENTS:
    It's him! It's d'Argenteuil!

STUDENT ONE:
    He hid Eric in his room.

STUDENT TWO:
    Under the bed, with his stamp collection.

STUDENT THREE:
>That's d'Argenteuil's third prisoner since September. . .

STUDENT FOUR:
>Tell us where you hid him.

KENT:
>You're being questioned, Pierre, reply.

D'ARGENTEUIL:
>I don't know what you're talking about. I haven't done anything.

LANCELOT: *who has been silent up to this point, rising quickly to his feet* What's the meaning of this? Why all these accusations? I don't understand you, Kent, creating such a climate of anxiety and anguish about the disappearance of Eric! After all, if he wanted to get away from this school, that's his business, isn't it? He's free to do as he pleases. Every one of us has wanted to escape this place at one time or another.

D'ARGENTEUIL:
>Of course, he'll come back, I'm sure of it. He may be down in the yard at this very moment. . .

KENT:
>But I tell you, it's not a matter of an escape but of a mysterious disappearance, I know all about it. . .

LANCELOT:
>After all, Eric has only been gone for one night. I too have occasionally disappeared for a night or two, but I wasn't necessarily in danger because of that.

KENT:
>Your insubordination astounds me, Lancelot! Really, what audacity! And what about the rules? And obedience?

LANCELOT:
I'm free to do as I please, to come and go as I please, even to run away if I please. I follow my own rules, not those of others.

KENT:
You will excuse me, Lancelot, but it is my duty to report your insubordination to the Superior. We cannot tolerate that sort of behaviour here!

LANCELOT:
What was your purpose in bringing us together here today? Your intentions don't seem to me entirely above suspicion.

KENT:
I can see you're preparing yourself very well to take over the chair of president next year.

LANCELOT:
I haven't always had the hightest esteem for you, I admit it. Yes, I'm anxious to replace you. I hope to perform a little more effectively than you have done. You don't preside, you crush!

KENT:
You've suddenly become very insolent. It's not like you. You were always so quiet, so silent, so sinister. . .

LANCELOT:
I'm not silent anymore. You're going to listen to me today, you're going to hear what I have to say.

KENT:
Indeed?

D'ARGENTEUIL: *worried*
Where is Eric?

STUDENT ONE:
You strangled him with your shoelace.

STUDENT TWO:
> You drowned him in the pond.

STUDENT THREE:
> You buried him in the bushes.

STUDENT FOUR:
> It's you. . . It's you. . .

KENT:
> In just a few moments, my friends, I shall reveal to you the name of the true culprit. And we shall honour him in our own fashion.

LANCELOT:
> I don't understand any of this.

D'ARGENTEUIL:
> We want to speak to the secretary and the vice-president about the disappearance of Eric.

LANCELOT:
> Yes, where is Stéphane? Why didn't he come to the meeting?

D'ARGENTEUIL:
> And Christian Ambre?

KENT:
> Stéphane will be here shortly, have no fear.

LANCELOT:
> The look on your face frightens me, Kent. You're up to no good. What are you trying to tell us? Is it possible that you've done away with Eric?

> *To the students.*

> Beware, my friends, Kent wants to make you his accomplices. A terrible threat hangs over your heads here today. . .

KENT:

Since you won't shut up, Lancelot, I'll have to shut you up. You're not in the habit of preventing the president of the class from speaking like this. You're lacking in discipline, I find. We must rectify that situation at once.

Rapping on the table.

You are witness, my friends, to the fact that d'Argenteuil and Lancelot are obstructing the business at hand. . . Seize them! Reduce them to silence!

The students throw themselves on LANCELOT and D'ARGENTEUIL and gag them.

Now, it's our turn to talk. Listen to me carefully, my friends. I have the pleasure of announcing to you that the hands of each one of you are stained with the blood of Eric. Yes, each one of you has committed this crime. The sin of one is the iniquity of the other. We are all members of the same community, are we not? It follows, therefore, that if one of us is guilty, we are all guilty, Isn't that right, José?

JOSE: *astonished*
I guess so. . . Yes. . .

KENT:

So, if the Superior asks you who killed Eric, you will say it was you. Right?

JOSE:

But that's not true.

KENT:

My friends, did he kill Eric. . . Yes or no?

STUEDENTS:

Yes!

56

KENT:

You don't understand, José? It's a game! Co-operate, there's nothing to fear. There's no point in resisting, you know. I'll have you gagged like Pierre d'Argenteuil if you resist. When the Superior comes to question us, we shall all declare ourselves guilty. He will be so confused that he will have no choice but to acquit every one of us. In that way, we shall be. . . innocent. Is that too complicated for you?

JOSE:

I understand. It's a game.

STUDENT TWO:

That'll be fun.

STUDENT THREE:

We're going to trick them all.

JOSE:

But if it's a game, then Eric is still alive?

KENT:

Dead, I tell you. Killed with a shovel, murdered, assassinated, not just once, but ten, twelve, thirteen times. . . Each one of us had a hand in his death!

STUDENT FOUR: *continuing what he vaguely believes to be a game* Shot at dawn. . .

STUDENT FIVE:

Crucified on the walls of the school. . .

STUDENT ONE:

Stoned to death!

KENT:

So! I have the proof now that we were all born to perform these thankless tasks, to kill, to crucify, to torture, yes, each one of us has it in him to carry out these cold blooded acts. I have the proof. . .

STUDENT ONE:

It was I who did it. It was cold that morning. I was in a bad mood when I woke up. I couldn't find my toothbrush. The bell was ringing for mass. I was in a terrible mood. I needed a victim. Anyone. Eric was there. I smashed my jug of water over his head. . .

KENT:

Well said, but your account lacks imagination. A bad mood is not enough. Something else is needed. Willfulness. . . Determination. . . A clear and resolute mind. . .

STUDENT TWO:

I was angry. Blind with anger. Eric was walking beside me. He was praying, I think. . .

KENT:

Even more than anger is needed! What is needed? I'll tell you. Coldness! Indifference! Yes, you don't understand. . . You feel cold, chilled right through to the bone. Rigid. Inflexible. Like a statue of ice. A murderous indifference possesses you, your heart and your soul are dry. . . Above all, at the moment of action, you rise above your own personal agony, you lose all touch with yourself!

STUDENT ONE:

But suddenly I was frightened. I thought I could hear footsteps in the dormitory. I couldn't continue. . .

STUDENT THREE:

Kent, it was you who directed me. . . I obeyed you. . .

STUDENT FOUR. *excited*

Yes, it was you, Kent, you acted in my place. . . I felt your hand directing mine. . .

KENT:

My friends, let me introduce you to the true murderer.

STUDENT FOUR:

> *STEPHANE enters, his face downcast, his hair dishevelled, so strangely distraught that they all gaze at him for a moment in silence.*

STUDENT FOUR:

What's the matter, Stéphane?

STEPHANE:

They found Eric's body in the bushes.

STUDENTS:

Eric's body in the bushes! Eric's body in the bushes!

KENT: *approaching STEPHANE and laying his hand affectionately on his shoulder* Poor Stéphane, what a blow this must be for you!

STEPHANE: *looking about the room*
What has happened to Lancelot and d'Argenteuil?

KENT:

Doing penance.

STUDENT SEVEN:

He's dead!

KENT:

How tired he looks! Can this really be the young man who killed Eric?

STUDENT TWO:

Was it you?

STUDENT THREE:

Was it him?

KENT:

Of course, it was him. He looks so sad. Let us applaud his performance, his magnificent courage! You can see how exhausted he is. . .

Pause.

KENT:

Applaud, I say! Applaud!

The students applaud, timidly at first, but then more vigorously.

Enough! Thank you! Prince Eric is dead. I present you with a bloody prince in his place. But this one is not smiling. He is sad and troubled. We must distract him a little from his grief.

STUDENT FOUR:
Bravo, Stéphane! You did well. . .

STUDENT FIVE: *timidly*
Bravo!

STUDENTS:
Bravo, Stéphane! Bravo!

KENT:

Everyone is in agreement, as you can see. We are all honoured to have performed this great deed with you. There are those who lead and those who follow. Willingly or not, we have all supported your action. You have nothing to fear, Stéphane. You are not alone. The hysteria of the mob sustains you now. We love you, we obey you, we are your devoted disciples.

STEPHANE: *rising angrily*
Is there not one of you capable of disapproving of my act?

STUDENT ONE:
We have nothing to add, Stéphane.

STUDENT TWO:
The matter is closed.

STUDENT ONE:
The president's decision is ours.

STUDENT THREE:
Eric is dead.

STUDENT FOUR.
Now we can choose another victim.

STUDENT FIVE:
I nominate d'Argenteuil.

STUDENT ONE:
He was condemned by our tribunal a long time ago.

STUDENT SIX:
He must be executed.

STUDENT SEVEN:
He is a threat to our school.

STUDENT THREE:
A bad example. . .

STUDENT ONE:
A source of scandal. . .

KENT:
Isn't it just as I told you, Stéphane, we are so much
their superiors that they will do anything for us.
They accustom themselves very quickly to crime, as
you can see. . .

STEPHANE:
They think you're playing. If they thought you were
serious, they would never follow you in this ugly
business. What gives you this power over them is
that they think you're playing with them, you
awaken the violence in their imaginations, you exalt
their folly with your own. . .

KENT:
Am I not very serious and calm?

STEPHANE:
Bring Lancelot to me. He'll listen to me. We are the only ones here capable of telling the truth.

KENT:
Bring Lancelot and d'Argenteuil!

STEPHANE: *to the students*
Listen to me.

STUDENTS: *shouting*
Murderer! Murderer!

STEPHANE: *crying*
You must forgive me. I've done a terrible, unspeakable thing. The reputation of this school is ruined forever. Listen to me...

STUDENT SIX:
It's too late.

STUDENT FIVE:
You're not capable of telling the truth.

STUDENT SIX:
You can only tell lies.

LANCELOT:
Please. Be quiet. Let Stéphane speak. He's the only one here with any integrity...

STUDENT SIX:
He no longer has the right to speak.

KENT: *climbing on the table*
Silence! You see, Luther. Nothing lasts. One moment, they admire you, the next, they're ready to spit on

you. That's what you inspire in them now: admiration and disgust. But isn't that precisely the role you chose for yourself? A very precarious role, if you ask me. Don't you regret it a little? Your best friends are turning against you. You possess nothing now. Honour does not exist. Isn't it just as I told you? Nothing endures.

LANCELOT:
What did you want to say to us? Speak, Stéphane.

STEPHANE: *shrugging his shoulders*
Nothing, Lancelot, nothing. I've forgotten.

LANCELOT:
Kent, if you think the gag will stop me from talking, you're mistaken. If no one else will speak, I will. . . Not always with words, because you don't hear them, but I'll find a way to defend myself against people like you. . .

KENT:
How clever he is! But I'm no more displeased with you today than I was yesterday. In fact, I rather enjoy your anger. I have to admit that it surprises me a little coming from you, but I appreciate it all the same. It does me homage.

LANCELOT:
You're on the wrong track, Kent. It's not possible to conquer others with such a hard heart.

KENT:
Oh God, everyone wants to put me on the right track! What is to become of me?

STEPHANE:
And on the snow. . . Eric's blood. . .

Suddenly, the SUPERIOR and CHRISTIAN AMBRE enter, carrying ERIC in their arms.

KENT is still standing on the table. The students press about him, as if to seek his protection. There is a long silence. The students stare at the SUPERIOR, who looks them over, one by one.

SUPERIOR:
Who killed Eric?

STUDENTS: *raising their hands and speaking in turn*
Me! Me! Me!

Only LANCELOT and D'ARGENTEUIL remain silent. They are standing in the middle of the room, looking a little guilty.

SUPERIOR:
Lancelot, d'Argenteuil, come here. . .

Act Two
Scene One

The same day, an hour later. The corridor outside the parlour. Standing a little apart from a group of students, STEPHANE and KENT are awaiting their turn to be called.

STEPHANE:

> So, now you've got what you wanted. Lancelot and d'Argenteuil are being questioned in our place.

KENT:

> Don't worry, your turn will come.

STEPHANE:

> Eric is dead. How can life go on as if nothing had happened? How can we continue to follow the schedule, with its appointed hours for recreation and study and visits, as if it were just another day? It's intolerable!

KENT:

> Lower your voice. Someone will hear you.

STEPHANE:

> And I suppose you'll have the nerve to see your mother today?

KENT:

> Why not? My mother would be terribly upset if she didn't see me. She adores me so! I'll see my mother and you'll see Hélène. It's shameful, I know, but what can we do, the Superior says that we must carry on as usual, as if nothing had happened. . . Didn't he make us promise to say nothing about the death of Eric? Not a word, until this evening. Don't forget that.

> *Pause.*

> Come on, Stéphane, don't look so sad. Eric is not alone. At this very moment, the priests of the house are all praying for him. Candles have been lit for the repose of his soul. Masses will be said for him. . .

STEPHANE:

> And his mother? Have you thought of the suffering of that poor woman?

KENT:

> Inconsolable mothers do not touch me. I don't have a bleeding heart like yours.

STEPHANE:

> She'll come to visit her son as usual this evening. They'll make her wait in the parlour. They'll tell her nothing. They'll make her wait. . . and then suddenly . .

KENT:

> Stop your brooding, you wear me out! Oh, you're so touching, so noble, those are qualities which I lack. Above all, emotion. . . And you have a real sense of drama: you see yourself in the place of others, you weep their tears, you suffer their

66

humiliations. You'd be an angel today if you hadn't
listened to me.

A voice is suddenly heard over the P.A. system.

VOICE: *in a monotone*
LOUIS KENT. PLEASE REPORT TO THE
PARLOUR. LOUIS KENT.

KENT:
They're calling me. My mother is waiting to smother
me with the terrible weight of her love. . .

Pause.

I'd like to say hello to your dear little sister
when she arrives.

STEPHANE:
Louis, stop it, please. I can't take any more of your
joking.

VOICE:
LOUIS KENT. LOUIS KENT.

KENT:
It sounds like the voice of the Last Judgement,
doesn't it?

STEPHANE:
Please, Louis. . .

KENT: *half-mocking, half-serious*
Don't forget, Stéphane. It's just another day. Hélène
is waiting for you. I'll see you later, my friend. . .

Scene Two

The parlour. KENT and his mother.

KENT:

Hello, Mother. Did you have a good trip?

He doesn't give her time to reply.

I've come a long way myself, you can't imagine.
But I feel fine. Winter is my season, it brings out
the cold in me, the suspicion, the pride. . . But why
do you stare at me like that? Do I look as if I'd lost
my mind? But I'm fine, I tell you, fine. Did you
bring me the books? And the money? I need money,
I have a fantastic project. . .

MOTHER:

Louis, my child. . .

KENT:

I had a dream. I was in prison. A prison of ice. Isn't
that strange?

MOTHER:

I brought you the books you asked for.

KENT:

A perpetual winter. I was terribly bored. You no
longer existed for me. No one existed. No one in
the world.

MOTHER:

Louis, you'll have to speak up, I can't understand you.

KENT:

Of course, you can't understand me, mother. That's
because I speak the language of terror.

He moves several steps away from her.

Oh, what a gloomy voice you have, Mother! How you bore me!

He turns abruptly back to her and sitting beside her, takes her hand.

How are you? Tell me all about yourself. How are you doing? I frightened you, didn't I? You don't like me to tease you like that?

MOTHER:

Louis, I don't recognize you anymore. You're changed so much during the past few weeks. Your father and I are very worried.

KENT:

Poor mother, I pity you, you'll be so unhappy.

Suddenly he changes his tone.

Is that all you have to say to me? I can't spend much time with you today. . . I have a lot of work to do, you understand. . .

MOTHER:

My darling. . .

KENT:

Oh, Mother, please don't start that. You know how I detest such precious words. You must excuse me, I'm in a hurry. . .

MOTHER:

Why don't you write to your father, Louis, why don't you ever think of us?

KENT:

I don't have the time.

He rises as if to leave, looking toward the door.

KENT:

> After all, I wasn't brought into this world just to please you. I'm not very pleased with it myself, you know.

MOTHER:

> Your father doesn't understand what is happening to you. You used to be so gentle. . .

KENT:

> Gentle! How do you expect me to be gentle today? How boring! Used to be! And when, may I ask, was that? Back in the days when you looked upon me as your possession?

MOTHER:

> Your father was so good to you. . . And I. . .

KENT:

> I'm sleepy.

MOTHER:

> You've become a stranger to your own family.

KENT:

> Yes, of course, that's how it is. A person grows up, doesn't he? Goodbye, Mother, I must leave now. someone is waiting for me.

MOTHER:

> Louis!

KENT:

> What is it?

MOTHER:

> You're hiding something from me, I can sense it.

KENT:

You have too much imagination, mother. I'm not hiding anything. I'm as transparent as daylight. Goodbye, Mother, you mustn't miss your train.

MOTHER:

Oh, the money! You said you wanted some money!

KENT:

Keep it, Mother, I'll get it the next time.

MOTHER: *calling her son, who has begun to withdraw, his hands in his pockets*
Your books, Louis, you've forgotten your books!

Scene Three

HELENE and STEPHANE, in another part of the parlour.

HELENE: *standing against a wall of bars, several feet from STEPHANE* I can't wait till you get home. I've done a lot of drawings for you.

STEPHANE:

I'm afraid I might be late for the Christmas holidays this year.

HELENE:

We'll take long walks together at night. I have so many things to tell you. And you must have things to tell me too. Just like the last time.

STEPHANE:

I'm not sure that I'll enjoy those walks anymore.

Pause.

71

STEPHANE:
> Have you been working hard at school?

HELENE:
> Hard enough. You'll see. I've made some progress on the violin.

STEPHANE:
> Hélène, listen, I'm afraid I may not be able to spend my holidays with you this year. I may not be allowed to leave school. A terrible thing has happened. . .

HELENE:
> Are you sick, Stéphane?

STEPHANE:
> Yes, that's it. I've been very sick. I'm not allowed to go out.

HELENE: *touching STEPHANE's hand*
> Your hand is burning. . .

STEPHANE: *recoiling*
> Don't touch me!

HELENE:
> But you'll get better.

STEPHANE:
> No, it's too late. You can't possibly understand. You're only a little girl.

HELENE:
> You wrote me such beautiful, sad letters. They all spoke of death.

STEPHANE: *gently*
> They didn't frighten you?

HELENE:
    No.

STEPHANE:
    Did you really understand what I was saying to you
    in those letters?

HELENE:
    Yes.

STEPHANE:
    I wasn't speaking only of death. . . I was speaking
    of. . . murder.

HELENE:
    Yes.

STEPHANE:
    And that didn't frighten you?

HELENE:
    No.

STEPHANE:
    It wasn't only a vague intention, Hélène. It was more
    than that, yes, I had the taste for it. It was an
    irresistible temptation. I actually wanted to do it.

HELENE:
    But you would never do that.

STEPHANE:
    Hélène, I did it yesterday. . .

        Pause.

HELENE: *calmly*
    It was just a bad dream. You couldn't do that,
    Stéphane, I know it. You're not as terrible as you
    say you are. Your letters were good for me, I always
    wanted to tell you that, but I didn't dare to. I sud-

denly came to know you through those letters. I
had always thought you were carefree and easy-
going, but your unhappiness made me see that I
was wrong.

Pause.

Because there wasn't only the unhappiness, you see. . .
There was also hope. . .

STEPHANE:
But there is no hope today. There is nothing like
that today.

HELENE:
Everyone has temptations like that, you said so
yourself. And perhaps it's true, perhaps there is a
sleeping monster in each one of us. I've thought a
great deal about that. Yes, perhaps it's true.

STEPHANE:
But you're only a child and you don't see the
difference between a harmless desire and its terrible
execution. You don't seem to understand that I
am quite guilty this time.

HELENE:
You know I can't believe that, Stéphane. You're
always taking the blame for other people. I'm sure
you haven't done anything wrong. You're just
imagining it.

STEPHANE:
Well, you'll soon see how guilty I am. When they take
me away to prison. When they charge me in front of
you. In front of the entire world. Then you'll see
that I was telling you the truth.

HELENE:
I'm sorry, Stéphane, I'm not as intelligent as you
are. I didn't always understand your letters. I tried

to understand them, but I didn't always succeed.
You're right when you say that I'm just a naive
little girl. But I'll change, I'll make an effort. . .

STEPHANE:
No, don't change. Please. I was just being cruel.
I didn't like to see you in church every day. I was
just making fun of you.

Pause.

I'm so afraid that I'll lose you, that you'll enter
a convent.

HELENE:
But even if I were in a convent, you wouldn't be
losing me.

STEPHANE:
You're all I have left now.

Pause.

Louis has humiliated me. . .

HELENE: quickly
You mustn't abandon him. I had a dream.

STEPHANE:
Tell me about it.

HELENE:
Louis was setting fire to the earth. . . No, I don't
remember. There was fire everywhere, all around
us. . . Oh, I'm sorry, I don't remember. You know I
can never remember my dreams.

STEPHANE:
Try to remember.

HELENE:

Louis. . . Louis. . .

STEPHANE:

No! I don't want to hear it!

HELENE:

Promise me you won't abandon him.

STEPHANE:

Even if I wanted to, that would be impossible.

HELENE:

He is even more unhappy than you.

STEPHANE:

You say that because you don't know anything about my unhappiness.

HELENE:

In my dream, we were all about to perish in a great river of fire. The earth was about to be covered with our ashes. But I didn't lose hope.

STEPHANE:

Hope! Of what use is hope? We have to learn to live without hope today, we have to live like silent madmen. Your dream is life, Hélène. There is nothing before us but fire and destruction.

HELENE:

But suddenly a fresh breeze touched my face. . . I heard birds singing in the distance. . .

LOUIS KENT enters, happy and smiling.

KENT:

May I join you? Your conversation intrigues me. . .

STEPHANE: *annoyed*

Visiting hours are almost over.

76

KENT:

> I left my mother to come and say hello to you, Hélène. You look very pretty.

STEPHANE:

> I'm not very pleased to see you here, Kent. Your presence is an embarrassment to us.

KENT:

> That's not very nice, Stéphane. You know very well that your friends are mine. Nothing can separate us in this life. We shall always be united, like two brothers. So why fear me?

STEPHANE:

> Because you have no scruples.

HELENE: *quietly*

> My brother often speaks of you in his letters.

KENT:

> But he tells me very little about you. He is very stingy with his secrets. How charming you are, you have a lovely smile! You're very much alike, you two. So sensitive and gracious! I'm glad to have had the opportunity to see you together like this. . .

> *The bell rings.*

HELENE:

> I have to leave now.

KENT:

> I'll look after your brother for you.

HELENE:

> I'll see you again soon.

KENT:

Who knows in what strange circumstances we may meet again. . . ?

HELENE:

Goodbye, Louis.

She withdraws, waving to the boys.

KENT:

So, here we are together again. What a lovely little sister you have! I should like to have her for my own.

STEPHANE:

Go away, Kent, I don't want to see you.

KENT:

What were you two talking about? Hell?

STEPHANE:

We were talking about you.

KENT:

But for me, destruction is not fire, you see. It's a cold, dark night. A winter night. The trees rigid with frost. The people shivering in their houses. The entire earth stiffening beneath the cold.

STEPHANE:

I'm going to turn myself into the Superior in a few minutes.

KENT:

You needn't bother. He's going to call you himself. He wants to question you. Imagine, you're one of the witnesses. . .

STEPHANE:

I'll tell him everything.

KENT:

But he won't believe you.

STEPHANE:

He'll believe me.

KENT:

The Superior is not interested in your confessions or your guilt. He has found his culprits. D'Argenteuil and Lancelot suit him perfectly. He has always suspected them of something. Now he thinks he was right.

STEPHANE:

They won't be accused in my place. I won't allow it.

There is the sound of a voice over the P.A. system.

VOICE:

STEPHANE MARTIN, PLEASE REPORT TO THE SUPERIOR'S OFFICE. STEPHANE MARTIN.

KENT:

You see, my plan is working perfectly. Everything is happening right on schedule. Fate is spoiling me.

Scene Four

Several days later. The visiting room of the prison, which resembles the parlour of the school.

KENT:

Oh, Stéphane, it isn't here that I hoped to meet you today! What a terrible blow this is!

STEPHANE:

> What's the difference between the bars which separate us here and those others which imprisoned us at school? You're kept at a certain distance from me here, that's all.

KENT:

> Don't be angry with me. After all, I came to visit you. And I shall come every Sunday.

STEPHANE:

> I don't want to see you.

KENT:

> It's your own fault, Stéphane. After all, there was no need to implicate yourself as you did. . .

STEPHANE:

> Lower your voice, someone will hear us.

KENT:

> Stéphane, you know I don't like to see you here. I miss you.

STEPHANE:

> You'll go on acting right to the end, won't you?

KENT:

> I'm sincere. I don't like the idea of you taking the blame for me. You had a choice. You could have betrayed all three of us. Why didn't you do it?

STEPHANE:

> I still had too much respect for you to do that.

KENT:

> But I didn't ask you to play the role of the martyr. Your obedience was all I demanded. This was the last thing I wanted for you, I assure you. I tried to speak to the Superior, but he wouldn't listen to me. You upset him with your story of the shovel and the

unpremeditated murder. . . Your confession of guilt
bewildered him, he no longer knows what to
think.

Pause.

The only reassuring thing is that he persists in
believing in your innocence and in accusing Lancelot
and d'Argenteuil of the crime. You may be saved
in spite of yourself.

STEPHANE:

Leave me at least the punishment I have chosen
for myself!

KENT:

Why did you say you killed Eric several times?

STEPHANE:

Because it's the truth.

KENT:

You musn't lose your mind, my friend. That could be
very dangerous for you.

STEPHANE:

Forget about me. I'm alright. It's Lancelot and
d'Argenteuil you should be thinking of. They're back
there, being punished in your place. Confessing my
crime wasn't enough. They didn't believe me. You
must speak up, Kent, you're the only one who can
convince them of my guilt. . .

KENT:

If they suspect Lancelot and d'Argenteuil, that's not
my business, I have washed my hands of those two!

STEPHANE:

Only you, Kent. . .

KENT:

> I won't do it.

STEPHANE:

> You must try at least to save d'Argenteuil and Lancelot from the unjust accusation which hangs over their heads. . . !

KENT:

> How could I do that? The Superior has evidence that d'Argenteuil and Lancelot were walking together in the woods at the hour of the crime, when everyone knows they should have been at mass with the other students. Strange, isn't it? You have to admit that they put themselves in a very delicate position. It's just as I said, the insubordination of d'Argenteuil will be their undoing.

STEPHANE:

> You know very well that their walk in the woods had nothing to do with our crime.

KENT:

> That's not what the Superior thinks. He sees a direct connection between their presence in the woods at that early morning hour and Eric's death. They might have murdered Eric during their walk. They might have attacked him, struck him, beaten him to death. . . I couldn't say myself. . .

STEPHANE:

> You must save them. They are innocent.

KENT:

> I have no interest in their innocence. And besides, the students have got used to the idea of their guilt. That's how they see it now. The Superior has never been very much taken with Lancelot and d'Argenteuil. How are you going to change the roles now?

STEPHANE:

Don't come to see me again, Kent. We have no more to say to each other. Our friendship is over.

KENT:

I'm going to save you from the punishment you seem so resolved to inflict upon yourself. I'm going to get you out of this place. In a few days you shall be free.

STEPHANE:

I don't want the freedom you speak of. Stay away from me, Kent.

KENT:

Don't forget what Hélène said. I'm very unhappy. You musn't abandon me.

STEPHANE:

I hate the very sight of you.

KENT:

Alright, hate me then. I would as soon be hated as loved. It is savage passions such as these that lend me a little life. Without your hatred, who knows, I might die.

STEPHANE:

No, you won't die, Kent. You'll only wither away like a rotten fruit.

KENT: *shocked*

You've lost your fine language, I see, that's a sign that I've truly begun to lose you. It's too bad, Stéphane, I wanted to protect you more than anyone.

Pause.

Do you eat well here? Do you sleep? Tell me about yourself.

STEPHANE: *coldly*
I'm fine. No drinking here, no smoking.

KENT:
You look tired. . .

STEPHANE:
That will pass. . .

KENT:
You'll soon be free, I promise you.

STEPHANE:
I don't want to leave this place. I'm quite alright here, thank you.

> *The bell rings. STEPHANE withdraws at once without even wishing his friend goodbye.*

KENT:
Stéphane, do you eat everyday?

Scene Five

A classroom. KENT and the students.

KENT:
And if you're asked at what time Lancelot and d'Argenteuil led Eric toward the woods, what will you say?

STUDENT FOUR:
At seven o'clock. They were walking toward the cemetery.

KENT:

How were they dressed?

STUDENT ONE:

D'Argenteuil was wearing a tweed coat.

STUDENT TWO:

And Lancelot was wearing a blue raincoat.

KENT:

Where were you when you saw d'Argenteuil and Lancelot heading toward the woods?

STUDENT TWO:

In the corridor. We were standing by the window smoking, waiting for the end of mass.

KENT:

And if the Superior asks you why you accused yourselves of the crime, what will you say?

STUDENT ONE:

That we did it for a joke.

STUDENT TWO:

For a laugh.

STUDENT THREE:

And to protect the real murderers.

KENT:

And who are the real murderers?

STUDENTS:

D'Argenteuil.

STUDENTS:

And Lancelot.

KENT:

Who killed Eric?

STUDENTS: *in chorus*
Lancelot! D'Argenteuil!

KENT:
And what was their motive?

STUDENTS:
Immorality! Immorality!

KENT:
And what about Stéphane Martin?

STUDENT THREE:
He was sleeping.

STUDENT TWO:
He was studying in his room.

STUDENT FOUR:
Stéphane Martin is innocent. Lancelot and
d'Argenteuil are guilty.

KENT:
How was Eric killed?

STUDENT ONE:
With a shovel.

KENT:
Who found the shovel?

STUDENT THREE:
I did.

KENT:
And where was it found?

STUDENT FOUR:
Near the cemetery.

KENT:
Who found Eric's body?

CHRISTIAN: *in a falsely innocent voice*
I did.

STUDENT ONE:
It was Christian Ambre.

STUDENT TWO:
It was Christian Ambre who killed Eric!

STUDENTS:
It was Christian Ambre!

STUDENT FOUR:
He wouldn't dare to kill a fly.

STUDENT TWO:
He's afraid of lightning. . .

STUDENT FOUR:
He's afraid of the Superior. . .

STUDENTS:
It's him!

STUDENTS:
Bravo, Christian Ambre!

STUDENTS:
Bravo! Bravo!

> *Laughing, the students raise CHRISTIAN onto their shoulders.*

STUDENT FOUR: *timidly approaching KENT*
I've always admired you, Louis.

KENT:
Oh?

STUDENT FOUR:
> Stéphane is gone. Would you let me be your new assistant?
>
> *In a low voice.*
>
> Would you let me be your friend?

KENT: *drily*
> We'll talk about it later. I'll have to think about it.
>
> *KENT leaves the room, his head high.*

Scene Six

> *The evening of the same day. D'ARGENTEUIL, LANCELOT and STEPHANE MARTIN in their prison cell.*

LANCELOT:
> What's the matter, Stéphane? Why do you look so sad? This cell is no smaller than the ones we live in at school. It's colder here, that's all. The winter seems longer than usual, but that doesn't matter. We're innocent, all of us, so why are you so frightened, Stéphane?

D'ARGENTEUIL:
> Lancelot is right, Stéphane, we should be proud of the fact that we refused to lie with the rest of the class. I can understand that Eric's death has upset you, it has upset all of us, it's as if we had lost a younger brother, but you aren't responsible for his death.
>
> *Pause.*

Believe me, Stéphane, you aren't.

STEPHANE:
Who then is responsible for his death?

D'ARGENTEUIL:
If I told you that, you would be very upset. You wouldn't believe me.

LANCELOT:
We think Kent did it.

STEPHANE:
Kent?

D'ARGENTEUIL:
Yes... Your best friend. I know how hard it must be for you to believe that, but...

STEPHANE:
I swear that it wasn't Kent. He was studying in his room. The murder took place in the woods, so there's no way that it could have been him.

LANCELOT:
But it couldn't have been anyone else.

STEPHANE:
Louis Kent is innocent, I swear it!

LANCELOT:
You accuse yourself to defend your friend, Stéphane. Your gesture is a noble one, but you must think of protecting yourself, not deliberately making yourself look guilty. That too would be a lie, you know. You are innocent.

STEPHANE:
Tell me then, where was I at the hour of the crime?

LANCELOT:
>At mass. I remember, you forgot your missal on the bench.

STEPHANE:
>No, it was the day before that I left my missal in the chapel. . . Saturday morning, I was with Eric Geoffroy. Kent will tell you that himself. Kent and Christian Ambre were studying in our room. I invited Eric to take a walk with me. We went as far as the cemetery gate. Eric was tired from walking. We sat down to rest beneath a tree. We smoked a cigarette. We didn't speak. It was snowing. I slid my hand into the pocket of my jacket and I found a knife and. . .

D'ARGENTEUIL:
>The proof of your innocence is that your version of the story changes each time you tell it. You're frightened, that's all.

STEPHANE:
>You don't understand then that I killed Eric several times?

D'ARGENTEUIL:
>No, whoever killed Eric killed him once, and it wasn't you. And it wasn't any of those hysterical children who threw their hands in the air and cried: "Me! It was me!" All those blind children applauding a murder frightened me. I've never seen anything so ugly in my life! Kent's presence in that room terrified me. . . For a moment, I actually thought I was looking at the devil. . .

LANCELOT:
>D'Argenteuil is right, Stéphane. You must regain your freedom in order to save the class. Louis Kent has bewitched the students. Someone has to stop him. Already, I've heard José repeating Kent's words without understanding them. The whole class is in danger, Stéphane, I can sense it. Kent wants to

turn us all into murderers and monsters, you must stop him before it's too late. He respects you. Who knows, he might listen to you, he might renounce his folly for you. You must speak to him.

STEPHANE:

But I tell you, *I* am the guilty one!

D'ARGENTEUIL:

You must ask Kent to come forward, to make a complete confession of his crime.

STEPHANE:

Louis Kent is innocent. I swear it.

There is a long pause, then he goes on sadly.

And what about you? How do you hope to save your-selves from the threat that is hanging over your heads now?

LANCELOT:

Confessing to a crime that you didn't commit won't help us, Stéphane. That's an illusion on your part. Only Louis Kent can establish our innocence by confessing his own guilt.

D'ARGENTEUIL:

And, of course, no one seriously thinks of accusing us. It's impossible. I have the feeling that we'll be out of here soon. . . Oh, it can't be true. Who could believe it?

LANCELOT:

The Superior will come to our aid. He knows very well that we're innocent. How could he let such a thing happen?

Long pause.

LANCELOT:

> Oh, I'm so sleepy all of a sudden! Do you want to sleep in the bed tonight, Stéphane? We can make room for you. . .

STEPHANE: *lighting a cigarette*

> I'm not sleepy, thank you. Good night.

> *LANCELOT curls up at the foot of the bed. D'ARGENTEUIL lies against the wall.*

D'ARGENTEUIL:

> I wish I could attend Eric's funeral.

LANCELOT:

> I haven't stopped thinking of him.

> *Pause.*

> Good night.

D'ARGENTEUIL:

> It's just like school. The cold, the bugs. There's nothing missing.

LANCELOT:

> Stop complaining and let me sleep, I'm tired.

D'ARGENTEUIL:

> Ringing bells, rotten food. I feel right at home.

STEPHANE:

> They're going to separate us soon. Maybe tomorrow.

> *There is the sound of a bell in the distance.*

LANCELOT:

> What bothers me is that my family is convinced of my guilt.

D'ARGENTEUIL:
>   And the whole class has set itself against me.

LANCELOT:
>   But that won't last. . .

D'ARGENTEUIL:
>   Good night.

LANCELOT:
>   I feel so dirty.

D'ARGENTEUIL:
>   I'm used to it. I never wash at school. The water is always frozen in the bottom of my basin in the morning.

LANCELOT:
>   I can't survive without my toothbrush.

D'ARGENTEUIL:
>   Be quiet now. I've heard enough from you. It's bad enough having to live with you in school without listening to your complaints all night long. . . in prison!

>   *Pause.*

>   Good night, Lancelot. Sleep well.

STEPHANE:
>   You don't understand then? Tomorrow we'll be separated?

LANCELOT:
>   Tomorrow we'll be free.

D'ARGENTEUIL:
>   I hear footsteps. . .

LANCELOT:
>It's a guard. Be quiet.

Scene Seven

A dream scene involving STEPHANE and HELENE

HELENE'S VOICE:
>Hello, Stéphane, are you there?

STEPHANE: *calling softly*
>Hélène? Hélène?

HELENE'S VOICE:
>Come and sit with me. It's such a nice morning.

STEPHANE:
>I can't go out. I've been confined to my room. The bars are too high. I can't see you, Hélène.

HELENE'S VOICE:
>I'm right over here. Come and sit with me.

STEPHANE: *moving towards her*
>Aren't you going to school this morning?

HELENE:
>I've decided to give up my lessons on the violin. I'm not very gifted, you know.

>*Pause.*

>Now we'll have more time to spend together, you and I. . .

STEPHANE: *sitting beside her*
What's that strange smell? Is something burning?

HELENE:
They're burning leaves in the park.

She opens a book on her knees.

Be quiet now, let me read.

STEPHANE:
Are you reading "The Adventures of Prince Eric?"

HELENE:
No. . . I'm reading "Electra." Don't you know it?

STEPHANE:
For four days now I've been confined to my room.

HELENE:
For four days now I've been waiting for you here.

STEPHANE:
I was severely punished.

HELENE:
I don't like mother to punish you. I told her not to
do that again. After all, you didn't do anything
wrong.

STEPHANE:
It was I who broke the mirror.

HELENE:
It was an accident, I'm sure.

STEPHANE:
No, not this time. I did it on purpose. I knew what I
doing.

HELENE:
> Stéphane, why won't you be quiet? I want to read!

STEPHANE:
> It all began so simply, with a phrase from Nietzsche,
> I think. . .

HELENE:
> I feel almost happy today.

STEPHANE:
> Is it true that you have a fiancé?

HELENE:
> Yes and no. My lover is invisible.

STEPHANE:
> I'd like to meet him.

HELENE:
> I'm almost happy, but I feel a little anxious. I think
> of you often, Stéphane.

STEPHANE:
> Oh, the sun. . . It's been such a long time since I
> saw the sun! Mother closed all the doors. It was so
> dark in my room.

HELENE:
> Yes, it's been a long time. But now you're with me.

STEPHANE:
> But who is that woman?

> *The silhouette of a woman can be seen in the
> distance.*

WOMAN:
> Eric! Eric!

HELENE:

And the sky is always so blue in October.

STEPHANE:

Did you hear her? She's calling him. . .

WOMAN: *her voice fading away*

Eric! Eric. . . !

STEPHANE:

Madame! Madame! I found his book bag near the cemetery. . .

WOMAN: *turning her back on him*

Yes, but it was empty. . .

She disappears and KENT enters, smiling, wearing the costume that he wore to play Creon at school.

KENT:

Hello, Stéphane, there's a storm coming up. How are we ever going to perform in the rain?

STEPHANE:

Our friendship is over, Louis. I no longer know you.

KENT:

Do you like my costume? Remember, I used to wear it for you at school.

STEPHANE:

You no longer exist for me.

KENT:

I know, I'm a frivolous, foolish creature. But what did you expect? Why did you listen to me? I'm so alone now without you. . .

STEPHANE:

> Goodbye, Kent.

KENT:

> The sky is so dark. It's so cold. Is it winter already?

STEPHANE:

> Will you ever stop acting? Will you ever take off the mask and reveal yourself for what you really are. . . A body without a soul?. .

KENT:

> You'll be sorry that you didn't have pity on me.

STEPHANE:

> I said goodbye, Kent.

KENT:

> I've arranged everything. You're free now. Lancelot and d'Argenteuil were kind enough to give themselves up in your place.

STEPHANE:

> What will happen to them?

KENT:

> How should I know? I have washed my hands of those two.

> *Pause.*

> The pain of death, no doubt. . .

STEPHANE:

> What will happen to them?

KENT:

> The voice of justice has spoken.

Pause.

Come with me now.

STEPHANE:
I can't. I feel so weak.

KENT:
You've lost a lot of weight.

STEPHANE:
Tell me the truth, Louis. Where are they?

KENT:
I told you, they're being tried in your place.

STEPHANE:
Oh! I slept too long. . .

KENT:
Don't you have your watch?

STEPHANE:
They took it from me yesterday.

KENT:
You have the support of the entire class. They have come here with me today. They're waiting for you outside. They rejoice with me at your liberation. We love you, Stéphane. How could we allow you to spend the rest of your life in prison?

STEPHANE:
If only. . .

KENT:
No, don't try to talk. You're too weak.

STEPHANE:
If only you had left me the burden of my guilt!

KENT:

> I leave you instead the burden of your innocence. Is that not preferable?

STEPHANE:

> You couldn't do me a greater disservice. What was that phrase of Nietzsche's you used to quote?

KENT:

> "Accept nothing, assume nothing, take nothing in, give nothing out in return."

STEPHANE:

> "An icy indifference to all."

KENT:

> It's time to leave. Come. The students are waiting for us in the yard.

> > *They move away and enter the yard. There they encounter a group of students dressed as Roman soldiers. At their head is ERIC, wearing his school uniform. He is pale but smiling, exactly as we saw him in KENT's room before his death.*

STUDENT THREE:

> You are free, Stéphane Martin.

STUDENT SEVEN:

> Lancelot and d'Argenteuil will be sentenced in your place.

STUDENT TWO:

> You are free, Stéphane Martin.

STUDENTS: *in chorus*

> You are free, Stéphane Martin!

STEPHANE:

> Stop! Stay away from me!

KENT:

Is this how you thank us for coming here to welcome you, Stéphane? That's not very generous of you. . .

STEPHANE:

Eric, help me, I'm a prisoner!

ERIC:

I'm sorry, Stéphane, I can't go out Thursday evening. I came to return your ticket for Phaedre. D'Argenteuil will go in my place.

STEPHANE:

You can keep the ticket, Eric. There won't be any holidays for me this year.

ERIC:

It's been a long time since my mother came to visit me. The last time she came, she brought me some flowers.

STEPHANE:

Eric, listen to me, I didn't have time to tell you. . .

ERIC:

I have to go now, Stéphane, it's time for my walk. The older boys are waiting for me in the yard.

STEPHANE:

Eric! Eric!

KENT:

Let's go, José, I want to talk to you. Goodbye, Stéphane, it's been fun. Thank you. Goodbye.

Scene Eight

In the prison cell. LANCELOT and D'ARGENTEUIL are still asleep.

STEPHANE:
Lancelot, d'Argenteuil, wake up!

LANCELOT murmurs in his sleep.

D'Argenteuil, I want to speak to you. . .

D'ARGENTEUIL; *in his sleep*
What is it? Is it time for mass?

STEPHANE: *standing and speaking to himself*
Oh God, perhaps they're right not to listen to me! I killed in a moment of violent passion and now everything is silent. No one can hear my voice, no one will listen!

> *Remembering ERIC's mother calling to her son in his dream.*

Eric? Eric? So you were only our first victim then? How many more will be there after you? The annihilation of your innocence has only just begun! Lancelot and d'Argenteuil will be charged in my place. Kent will find someone else to replace me. You will die again, Eric! I can still hear the voices of those students who killed with joy, their laughter penetrates the walls of the prison. "Applaud!" says Kent, and together they raise their childish voices in noisy applause.

> *We hear the distant cheers of the chorus. They grow in intensity then abruptly cease.*

How many more victims will there be after you, Eric?

Once again, the invisible chorus cheers, loud and long.